With You Always, Little Monday

Geneviève Côté

Harcourt, Inc. • *Orlando   Austin   New York   San Diego   Toronto   London* • *Printed in Singapore*

One summer, on a clear Monday night, the forest animals found a baby rabbit fast asleep in the moonlight.
They called him Little Monday.

Little Monday and his new friends loved to play games and explore the forest.

But sometimes, in a quiet moment, Little Monday would sit alone and wonder who his mommy might be.

One day he decided to look for her.

Little Monday went to see Swan first. She was gentle and graceful, and Little Monday really wanted her to be his mommy.

But Swan said she wasn't.

"Never mind," said Little Monday. "I can't swim like you, anyway."

He asked Owl next. She was very wise. Little Monday would love to have a very wise mommy! But Owl said she wasn't his mommy, either.

"Never mind," said Little Monday. "I could never stay awake all night like you, anyway."

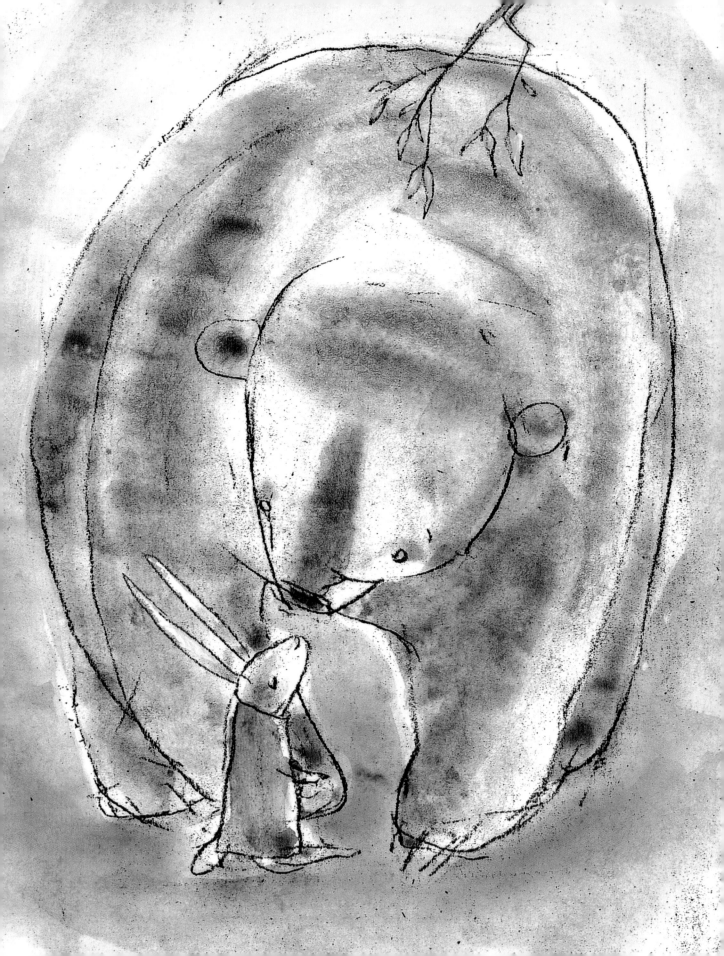

Around lunchtime, Little Monday found Bear by a blueberry bush. She was big and strong and could protect Little Monday from anything in the world.

But Bear said she wasn't his mommy.

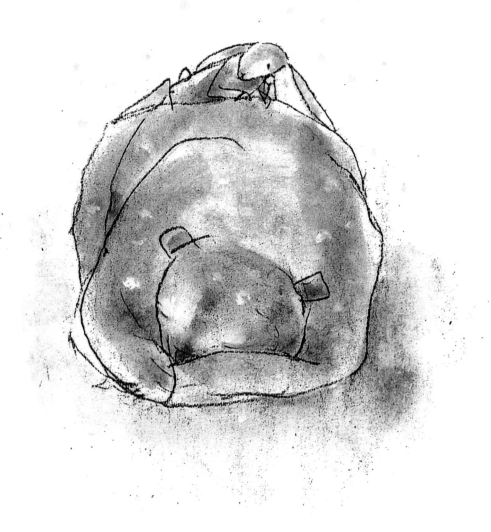

"Never mind," said Little Monday. "I couldn't sleep all winter long like you, anyway."

Off he went to ask Chipmunk. She was always jumping and dashing. It would be fun to have a mommy like that!

But Chipmunk said she wasn't his mommy.

"Never mind," said Little Monday. "I could never climb up all those trees like you, anyway."

Little Monday spotted Skunk and nearly ran away. (Skunk could smell *very* stinky.) But then he thought he'd better ask her, just to be sure. Skunk said she wasn't his mommy.

"Never mind," said Little Monday.
Frankly, he was relieved.

It was getting late when Little Monday
asked Raccoon, Bat, Turtle, and Fox, then Otter,
Heron, and Frog . . .

but none of them was his mommy.
Little Monday felt like giving up.

In the fading light, Little Monday curled up in the ferns and closed his eyes.

Maybe tomorrow I will find her, he thought as he fell asleep.

Late that night, Little Monday awoke with
a start. Was someone calling his name?

He looked left and right, front and back.
Finally, he looked up....

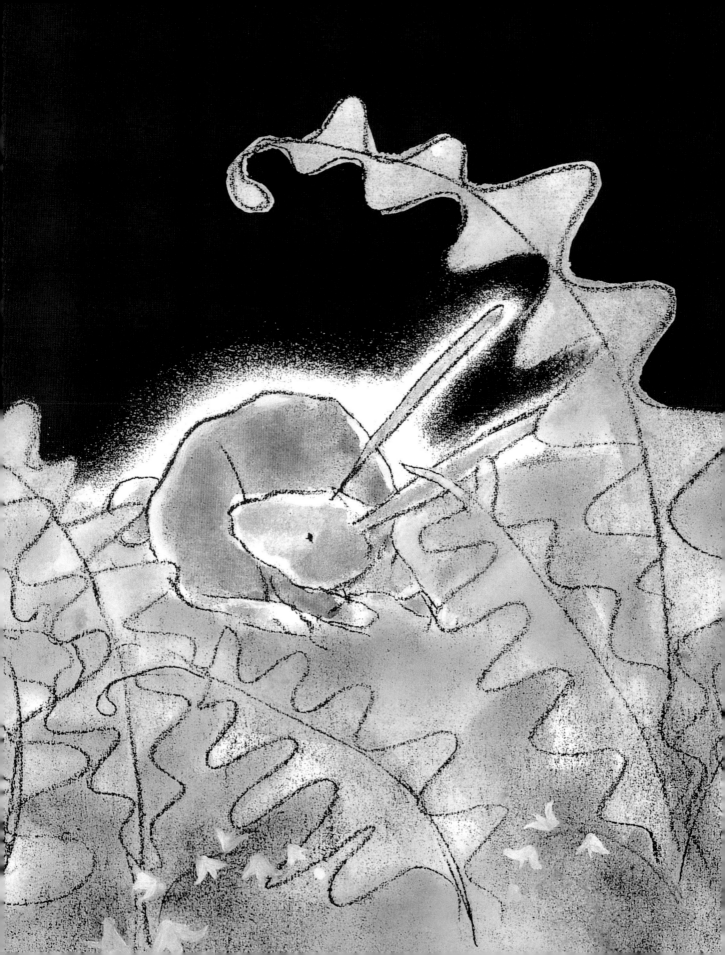

And there, in the big bright moon, a rabbit was smiling at him.

Little Monday rubbed his eyes. "Could you be my mommy?" he called. "But you're so far away, up there in the sky!"

"I may not always be nearby, Little Monday, but I watch over you and light your way in the forest. Even on the darkest nights, even when you can't see me, I'm always with you."

Little Monday smiled. He could feel a moonbeam on his cheek.

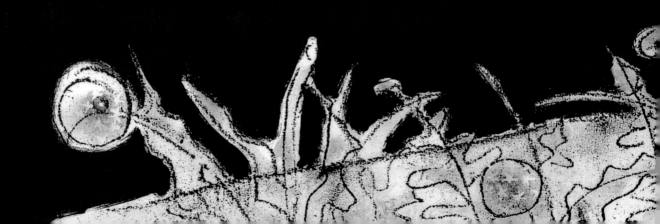

"Wake up, everyone!" Little Monday called. "Can you see my mommy? She's been right here all along!"

Little Monday and his friends stayed up very late that night.

Then, one by one, the other forest
animals drifted off to sleep.

Little Monday tried to stay awake with
his mommy as long as he could....

And when he closed his eyes at last, he heard a whisper in the moonlight:

"Good night, Little Monday. Sleep tight."

AUTHOR'S NOTE

Montag, lundi, lunes, lunedì, maandag…

In many languages, *Monday* means "day of the moon." Look carefully at the full moon. Do you see the shadow of a rabbit running across the sky? Or maybe she is sitting quietly in the moonlight? From China to the Americas, people around the world have celebrated this gentle presence for thousands of years.

The moon rabbit can still be seen today, reminding us that no one is ever truly alone in the night.

For everyone I love,
and for anyone who ever doubted
the promises of dawn
—G. C.

Requests for permission to make copies of any part of the work should be submitted online at www.harcourt.com/contact or mailed to the following address: Permissions Department, Harcourt, Inc., 6277 Sea Harbor Drive, Orlando, Florida 32887-6777.

www.HarcourtBooks.com

Library of Congress Cataloging-in-Publication Data
Côté, Geneviève.
With you always, Little Monday/Geneviève Côté.
p. cm.
Summary: Little Monday, a baby rabbit, searches for his mother with the help of his woodland friends.
[1. Rabbits—Fiction.   2. Forest animals—Fiction.
3. Mother and child—Fiction.]   I. Title.
PZ7.C82424Wit   2007
[E]—dc22   2006016829
ISBN 978-0-15-205997-2

First edition
H G F E D C B A

The illustrations in this book were done in mixed media.
The display type was set in Melanie BT.
The text type was set in Worcester Round.
Color separations by Colourscan Co. Pte. Ltd., Singapore
Printed and bound by Tien Wah Press, Singapore
This book was printed on totally chlorine-free Stora Enso Matte paper.
Production supervision by Christine Witnik
Designed by Linda Lockowitz